Christmas with Snowman Paul

Written by Yossi Lapid
Illustrated by Joanna Pasek

ISBN 978-0-9993361-0-6

To Nils, Maria and their
wonderful families

Paul's heart is made of frozen snow,
His feelings, though, are quick to show.

The other day, I found him there
Mumbling sadly: "It is not fair!"

"Hey, Paul" I said, "What's going on?
Here, have a lick before it's gone!"

"Oh, no!" snapped Paul, "Christmas is near,
And I have nothing much to cheer...

You'll have your fancy meal inside...

You'll carol by the fireside...

You'll light your shiny Christmas tree...

You'll chat with everyone, but me.

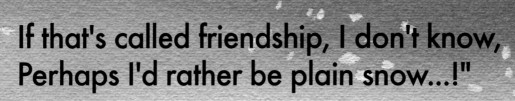

If that's called friendship, I don't know,
Perhaps I'd rather be plain snow...!"

"You're right!" I said, "I'll find a way —
Let's see what others have to say..."

I ran inside and rallied all,
To see what we can do for Paul.

We formed a circle, all around

And a solution was soon found.

It was, perhaps, a little strange,
But nothing, we could not arrange!

On Christmas Eve the stars were bright,
And everyone was out of sight.

Paul was inside, now fully able
To sit at our festive table.

Then, after dinner, we played games,
With Paul, still shielded from the flames.

And when old Santa made his call,
He had a special gift for Paul!

Merry Christmas!

Made in the USA
Middletown, DE
28 October 2018